THE DOG WHO LOVED RED

First American Edition 2011
Kane Miller, A Division of EDC Publishing

Text and illustrations © 2006 Anitha Balachandran
First published by Scholastic India 2006

For information contact:
Kane Miller, A Division of EDC Publishing
PO Box 470663
Tulsa, OK 74147-0663
www.kanemiller.com
www.edcpub.com

Library of Congress Control Number: 2010931033

Printed and bound in Malaysia by Tien Wah Press Pte. Ltd.
1 2 3 4 5 6 7 8 9 10

ISBN: 978-1-935279-83-9

THE DOG WHO LOVED RED

Anitha Balachandran

Kane Miller

A DIVISION OF EDC PUBLISHING

Raja loved r.e.d.
and Raja loved chewing.

He chewed Mrs. Lal's
r.e.d shawl.

"Raja!!
NO!"

He chewed Tanvi's **red** shoes.

"Raja! Stop it!"

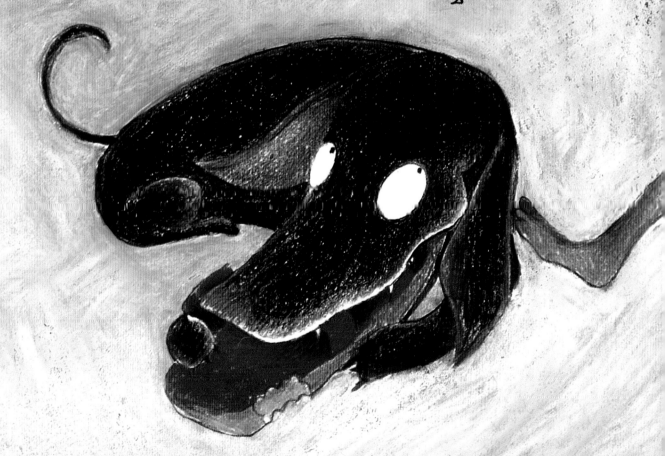

He chewed Mr. Lal's
gray and **red** socks.

"Out! OUT!"

"Come here, Raja!"
said Tanvi,

and she took Raja
to the park.

In the park,
Raja usually played
with Champ.

Champ was white
with black spots.

They liked to play
with an old red ball.

But today, Champ was very quiet.

"Is something wrong?" asked Raja.

"The ball's lost," said Champ, sniffing around the green bushes.

"I can't find it anywhere."

Raja asked
the gray pigeons
if they had seen it.

"Ba... ba... blue blah?"
asked a small, fluffy pigeon.
"No, not a blah, it's a BALL,
and it's RED, not blue," replied Raja.

Raja asked
the orange striped
kitten if she had seen it.

"Purrrrr ... a bowl?
Like a bowl
of milk?"

"No, no, not a bowl.
A ball," sighed Raja.
Cats could be silly sometimes.

Luckily, Raja had red radar.
He could find
ANYTHING red.

He could spot ALL
the red beetles and bugs
in the garden.

And in Mr. Mehta's backyard,
he could see the red ball!
Mr. Mehta lived next door. Mr. Mehta
hated dogs. He always turned on his
big **blue** hose and chased
them away.

Raja didn't like getting wet.
And Raja didn't like Mr. Mehta.
But before Tanvi could stop him,
    Raja slipped under Mr. Mehta's
        violet gate,

squirmed up
the dusty gray driveway,

leapt onto
the green cooler,

slid flat
under the shiny silver car ...

Great! Got it!

"AAAIEEE! YOU ... YOU ... LITTLE ... !!!"
Mr. Mehta yelled and charged.
Raja dodged and ran.

Mr. Mehta stood in front of the gate in his bright yellow shorts.

Only one way out—

Raja dived into the **brown** flowerpots,

scattering them left and right, clambered up the white bed sheet,

jumped onto the **maroon** mailbox, ran along the top of the prickly hibiscus hedge,

bit through a **pink** plastic net and was **back** in the Lals' garden!

MAIL

Covered with sticky **brown** mud,
bits of **pink** netting,
squashed flowers,
a **blue** cloth
and a **peach** sock,

Raja made his
way to the park.

The **red** ball was in his mouth.

"You did it!"
said Champ.
He thumped his tail,

"Aaoo...

aaaooo!"

and ran
around
in circles.

"Raja,

you're a hero!"
said Tanvi, clapping
her hands and giggling.
"A very odd
and colorful hero!"

"Woof!"
said Raja happily.

"And do you know what heroes
like you get as a reward?"

"Wuff?"

"A BATH!"